CHOCOLATE COVERED FROG LEGS

Poems by
Justin Matott

Drawings by
John Woods, Jr.

SKOOB BOOKS

LONDON   FRANCE   UNDERPANTS

For my nephews; Julian and Kingsley.
I hope you will enjoy tons of Chocolate Covered Frog Legs!
—JM

For Justin Matott, my mentor, hero and favorite friend.
—JW

(Okay, truth is John Woods Jr. never submitted his dedication,
so Mr. Matott wrote it. What a MEGADORK!)

HEY, YOU SNOOZE, YOU LOSE... HE HAD HIS CHANCE!
—JM

WHATEVER!
—JW

Requests for permission to make copies of any part of the work should be mailed to:
Permissions Department, SKOOB BOOKS, Box 261183 Littleton, CO 80163.
Library of Congress Cataloging-in-Publication Data
Chocolate Covered Frog Legs written by Justin Matott; illustrated by John Woods, Jr. – 1st ed. p. cm.
Summary: Assorted quips and poems about the everyday stuff of life.
ISBN 1-889191-06-X {1. poetry. I. John Woods, Jr. 1954—   ill. II. Title
First edition   A B C D E
Printed in Hong Kong
To contact Mr. Matott regarding his work,
please write to SKOOB BOOKS, a division of BOK BOK BOOKS,
or go to www. justinmatott.com.
Email Matott in care of RandomWrtr@aol.com.
For Mr. Woods, please email: jdwoodsjr@comcast.net
If you are interested in a school presentation by Justin Matott, please go to
www.author-illustr-source.com/justinmatott.htm

CHOCOLATE COVERED FROG LEGS

THE FIRST POEM

The first poem in this book
should have a good hook,
something to draw you right in.

So I thought and I thought
until an idea I caught,
one I thought might make you grin.

When you rhyme every word,
stay away from the absurd.
If you make up words, that's cheating.

So I have to make sense,
which can make me so tense,
on the ground my head I'll be beating.

If you want a good reader,
then be a good writer-
if you're boring your reader will yawn.

So use words exciting
and thoughts so inviting,
they'll read it from dusk until dawn.

I think I finally got it,
and now that I've thought it,
I'll give you this book of poems.

They're fun and quite wacky,
and some a bit tacky,
so read it first when you are alone.

Ahem! Without further ado
I will entertain you
with subjects that fit us so well.

There are underwear tales,
and poems by the pails
full of words that'll ring a kid's bell!

A PEN PAL

My friend just moved away.
We promised that we'd write
each other once a day.
I wrote to him tonight.

Dear Pen Pal,
I mean Frankie,
why did you move away?
I think about the football games
we played most every day.
How we used to chase the dogs,
and how the dogs chased us.
I remember when we sat together
on our big school bus.
I wish you hadn't moved away,
and that you lived next door.

Dear Pen Pal,
I mean Frankie,
Now I miss you even more!

9

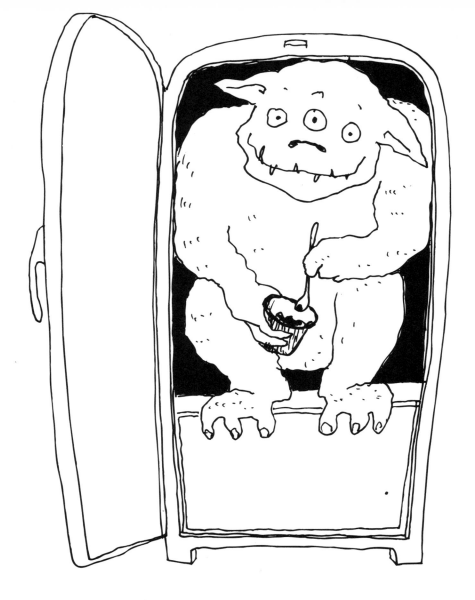

LURKING IN THE FRIDGE

Deep inside my refrigerator,
there lurks this awful thing!
When I open up the door,
my nose just starts to sting...
It's smelly and looks really bad,
has green hair and a mole.
It slithers around in the back,
and lives in a dark hole.

But now I'm really hungry,
so I'll take a risk I think…
I plug my nose. I hold my breath.
"Oh boy, that fridge does stink!"
"What is it?" I must ask someone,
it can not be quite edible.
Then I put it in my mouth,
the taste of it's incredible…

and when it's in my mouth,
I hear this little scream.
Sitting on that lump of food
like a mass of old ice cream,
is a funny little creature
that grew out of some mold.
It grabbed onto my fork,
then pulled it with a scold;

"THAT FOOD IS MINE!
        MOLDY LIVERWURST!"
"YOU CAN'T HAVE IT,
        I HAD IT FIRST!"

It's slick and it's slimy,
it's cold and it's grimy,
just like an awful dream.
That refrigerator monster
scurried off with my ice cream!

11

A MOUSE IN MY SOCK

There's a mouse in my sock.
How he got there's a mystery.
But when I step down,
that mouse will be history.

13

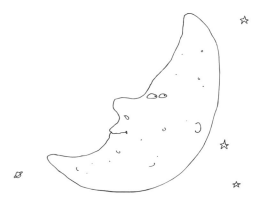

THE MOON MAN

One evening as I watched the sky,
I kept my eye on a funny face.
I'd seen it somewhere before.
But it was one I simply couldn't place.
Then my brother told me something,
"There's a big, mean moon-man!"
He told me that the moon-man had
a big, mean moon-man plan.
He was going to take over our earth…
He was going to come invade.
Soon we might have
a mean moon-man parade.
But how could he leave the moon,
when his face is clearly half?
I scratched my head and thought,
my brother bent and laughed,
"The moon's his head, you goofball …"
my brother said so smartly.
"His body's just invisible.
What you see is only partly."

14

"His toes touch down in the ocean blue.
His fingers graze our land.
When volcanoes rock and rumble,
it's what the moon-man planned.
Yes, he's been here while you're asleep.
And he will come back soon."
My brother told me so many things
my head began to swoon.
The next day in my classroom
as we studied outer space,
I asked the questions I had held
about the moon-man's face;
"Please, teacher, will you tell me,
is the mean moon-man really real?"
My teacher told me he was cheese,
could make a delicious meal
Now I don't know whom to believe.
Guess I'll just blast off to space.
I'll find out for myself someday,
about that moon-man face...

THAT JUST TAKES THE CAKE

When I grow up I'm going to live
in a house made of scrumptious cakes,
with a frosting roof and icing walls,
where the gutters blend milk shakes.
A home SWEET home it will be
of chocolate and of cream.
My house will be my favorite place
to fulfill my every dream!
Oh, I have a major sweet tooth,
so a pastry house I'll make.
Yes, someday I will bake it,
and that will take the cake!

16

MY HATS OFF TO YOU

Hats off! Hats off!
Let's throw them up!
Let's throw them really high!
Let's let them reach the highest yet.
Way high up in the sky.

17

LIFE IS ALL ABOUT BALANCE

Life is just a tightrope
between one thing and the next.
Is it any wonder
that so often we are vexed?

Don't be extreme on the left,
or extreme on the right!
If you lose your balance,
you'll slip right out of sight.

SODA POP BLUES

Soda fizz, soda fizz
bubbling in my nose.
I took a huge gulp of pop,
then I giggled I suppose...

The soda jumped up from my mouth,
then out of my nostrils shot...
That soda made a nice big stream,
then left an ugly spot.

MY MONSTER

There is this hairy monster
who lives beneath my bed.
He lies down there and mumbles.
His snores hurt my poor head.
He sleeps when I'm awake
and is awake when I'm asleep.
And when my room is very dark,
he starts to sneak and creep.

He's looking for a midnight snack.
He just might eat my toes.
And if he's really hungry,
he'll eat my ears, then nose.
I tried to tell my brother
'bout the monster under there.
He tells me, "JUST BE QUIET!"
He doesn't seem to care.

So even though I share a room,
with my older brother geek,
I feel all alone
with an under-bed monster freak!

That monster's scary, hairy, mean.
He grunts and sniffs and wheezes.
Even though it's my bedroom,
he does just as he pleases.

I have to do something 'bout him,
because I just can't sleep.
I can hear that monster breathing,
I will defeat that creep.

I must think of a great thing
to foil that monster's plan
to beat me up and eat me.
I'm scared, oh man, oh man.

You see I'm in a bunk bed,
on the top right near the ceiling.
My older brother's on the bottom,
which is even less appealing.
Except wait…, the monster has to get him
before he can get to me.
I'll get him to like brother meat,
I think that is the key.
My brother's feet are stinky,
I think monsters might like his pew,
geez, I am just skin and bones,
and my brother could lose a few.

The monster just watches us,
from his under bed hiding place.
And when he sees my brother,
it'll put a smile upon his face.
Yes, that is a good, good plan,
my brother will get eaten,
and then, oh then I think,
that monster will be beaten.

But what if monster's still hungry,
and he begins to hiss?
Maybe I should plan
to give him my annoying sis.

But he can't eat my brother,
and though sis is sometimes bad,
I deep, deep down still like them
and think of fun we've had.

So what if we three joined together
to chase that monster out?
We could battle him and beat him,
yes, we would scream and shout.
So I start to describe him,
and my brother starts to shake,
When our bunk beds begins to move,
they really start to quake.

My sister is so curious,
she crosses the hall to see
why brother and I are whispering,
then she climbs in bed with me.

All three of us start talking
about the awful hairy brute,
who lives beneath our bunk beds,
with my popgun, him we'll shoot.
And then we'll tie him to a chair
and we will torture him,
we'll fight him hard and tear him up,
rip him limb from limb!

At last a soft crying sound,
reveals a monster's scare.
He snuck out of our bedroom,
wearing brother's underwear.

He runs down the long hall,
we follow him and shout,
he jumps from stair to stair to stair,
just trying to get out.

And last I heard, that monster
was living next door with the Spits,
under the neighborhood bully's bed,
giving *him* bad nightmare fits.

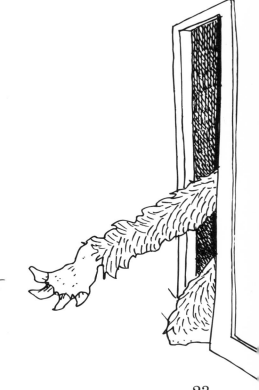

IF MICE RULED THE WORLD

In my house it's backwards.
The pets I call my own
are the ones that in most houses
make people moan and groan.
My favorite pet's a mouse.
(My next favorite's a spider),
but EWWW sometimes the cat gets in,
and I must run and hide her!

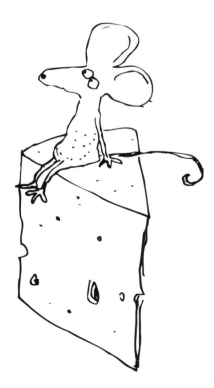

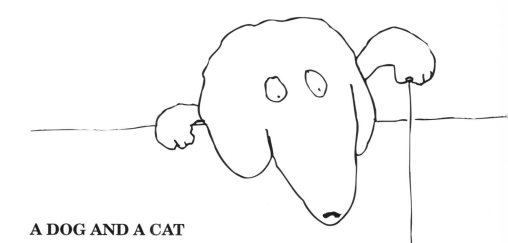

A DOG AND A CAT

There are two little pets
living in my house.
One likes to chase toys,
one likes to chase a mouse.

They play with each other,
though they aren't supposed to.
They are the best of friends,
and here is what they do;

Though they both have a basket,
they sleep next to each other.
They act like one's the sister
and the other is the brother.

They fight like cats and dogs at times.
Then they're friends once more.
My cat and dog are funny that way,
as they chase out our back door.

SPACE CADET

My head is sometimes empty.
I cannot find a thing.
I think I might have set it there.
And then to mind I bring,
a thought that I cannot catch,
and my head is awfully blurred.
I'm sure I had just put it there,
but that seems so absurd.
How can I forget so quickly?
It now seems a huge mystery.
I guess I'm just a space cadet,
and my memory is now history.

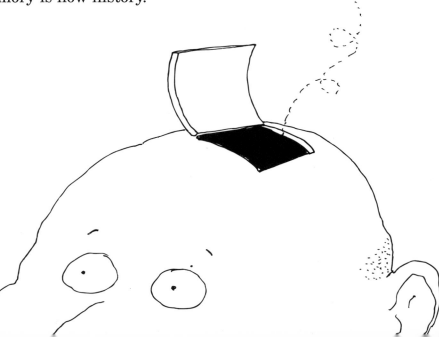

THERE ONCE WAS...

There once was a man
who lived up on a hill.
He was the mean ogre
who pushed Jack and Jill.

Of this mean man
most folks were afraid.
He tormented kids
when near his house they played.

Once a group of children,
tried to go across his place.
He yelled at them so loudly,
took the smile right off each face.

So back to Jack and Jill,
What happened to those two?
Well, this is not about them,
so that will have to do.

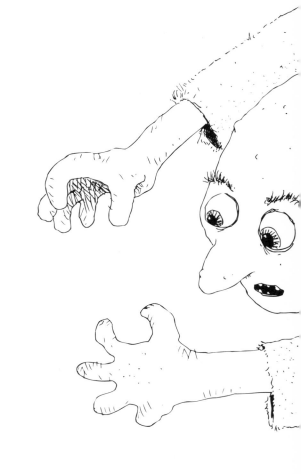

27

MY LAUNDRY BASKET

We have a bright green basket
to carry clothes to wash,
I use it as my space machine
when I slide down the stairs, "OH GOSH!"

"OH GOLLY, OH GEE WHIZ",
I'm flying through the air!
I fly so high I'm falling
into a pile of underwear!

And now the basket is a car
in a race, goes round and round.
I'm driving up and down the hall
and making a HUGE sound!

Then I turn it over,
pretend I'm stuck in jail.
I rock it and I roll it,
from this prison I must bail.

And then my sister walks in the room
"Hey! Let's feed the freak!"
She sits atop the basket.
Oh, my sister's such a geek!

CREATURE FEATURES

Vampires, werewolves,
Frankenstein, ghouls,
ghosts and witches,
spooks and fools!

Monsters everywhere,
"not normal" creatures.
Each is distinct
with individual features.

And these are just my siblings here at my own home.
If I want to be scared, I don't have too far to roam.

I am a human,
but the only one here,
the rest of my family
will cause you great fear.
My dad is a goblin,
my mom is a ghoul,
we live in a cabin
right down by my school.

Sometimes we are normal,
sometimes weird we seem.
My family is so strange
I just want to scream!
What an odd family,
glad there are no clowns!
They are rarely funny,
they only bring me frowns.

There's nothing as scary
as a clown or a mask.
Finding unique creature
features, is an easy task.
Then in runs our platypus,
his name's Friendly Fred.
And platypus's brother Bob
is there all dressed in red.

Most families have a dog or maybe a cat,
that wouldn't do, no we wouldn't do that.
For we are the "Weirdoes", with many strange features.
Yes, we are so different, a house full of creatures.

A PLACE TO WRITE

Once there was a place I went to write my stories down.
A place I called my own. A place right in my town.
No one there to see me, and no real conversations.
A place to concentrate, on all my writerly occasions.

That place was in my bathroom,
until my brother moved back home.
Now he's in there all the time,
I'll find a new place to work my tome.

YOUR THINKING CAP

I have this cap I found one day, and set it on my head.
And ever since that fateful day, telling stories earns me bread.

Ideas rushed into my brain, I had to get them out.
"SOMEONE GIVE ME PAPER!" I began to scream and shout.

Yes, for so long I went around with stories dull and boring.
But when I got my thinking cap, my stories started soaring!

So you go get a cap and put it on, to hold your thoughts in tight,
then get a pencil and a pad and just begin to write.

So soon you will realize your stories are surprising,
that thinking cap has helped you, your grades now are rising.

PIANO LESSONS

The plink-plink-plink of off-tune songs
is what I do the best!
And I have to learn at least three songs
for my next recital test.
I play chopsticks with great skill,
and even use both hands.
But I have to learn another song
for my piano teacher's plans.

MUSIC

My favorite thing to do
is listen to a song.
And when the radio is loud,
I often sing along.
I sing most in the shower,
I hum both day and night,
I like to hear the music play,
it makes me feel just right.

UNDERWEAR? UNDERWHAT?

A boxer or a brief,
is a boy's choice for down there.

But that isn't what is bugging me
about my underwear!

No, my problem is the color,
my undies are all pink!

Please let me explain this,
it's just not what you think.

You see, I did the laundry last,
threw in colors with the white.

A really blood-red sweatshirt,
mixed in, made my mom uptight!

"NO! I WILL NOT GET YOU NEW ONES!"
Mom yelled and she was mad…

But I just can't wear pink undies,
so I'll go beg my dad!

CREEPY CRUD

I sneeze, I shake, I cough, I ache,
I don't like the flu at all!
It seems that every wintertime,
or sometimes even fall,
the creepy crud hops on to me,
and makes me feel so bad.
I cannot go to school today,
and that just makes me mad.

The reason I am mad 'bout that
is today they're having fun.
We worked so hard this school year
and now a half is done.
Of all the times to get the crud,
this day is just not it!
There's games and parties in my class,
while at home I cough and spit.

MY FUNNY BONE

I bumped my elbow on a chair.
It tingled quite a bit.

A shocking little feeling,
and it just wouldn't quit.

Why do they call it funny?
It doesn't feel too good.

I wish that when I did that
my elbow was just wood.

"PICK YOUR BRAIN?"

What a weird thing to say,
when you need someone's advice.
To suggest you'll pick a brain
just doesn't sound that nice.

And to peel your eyes
when you're watching out?
When someone says that,
it makes me want to shout!

Just seems to me like pain,
the visuals these words evoke.
Like when someone says that one
about a sharp stick and eye poke.

The words we use paint pictures
in the minds of those who hear.
Why would you say to someone,
"Hey, please lend me your ear?"

These words when used together
just make me kind of queasy.
To pick a brain or peel an eye,
is disgusting and not easy.

ANOTHER MOUSE IN MY SOCK

My mom got me tube socks,
which I keep in my drawer.
I only wear two at a time,
and the next day, wear two more.

This morning I had a big surprise,
when I slid into my sock.
Tiny toe holes were apparent
and then that tube sock talked.

Well, actually the sound I heard
was really just a squeak.
It was getting louder,
a mouse started to speak.

A little mommy mouse,
had made my sock her nest.
I didn't use that tube sock
that morning when I dressed.

And now my dresser drawer
is full of little squeaky mice.
So before I slip socks on my feet,
I always do look twice.

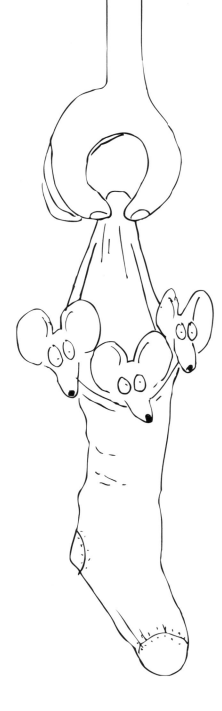

39

MY BULLY

I was swinging on the swings one day
just minding my own affairs,
when a mean kid pushed me hard,
caught me unawares.
For thirty weeks right after that
he bothered me each day.
When all I wanted was some peace
and a safe place just to play.
Then one day I'd just had it,
I couldn't take much more.
So I found a bigger kid
told him what I'd need him for.
The next day we were swinging
when my bully came to call.
He pushed my swing again hard,
he tried to make me fall.
So then my even larger friend
gave my bully quite a push.
He chased him past the slide
then tossed him in a bush!
My bully went off running
to find an even bigger friend.
The next day they both came back
some help that guy would lend.
They challenged us to a fight,
but my bully's friend was huge.
So we went searching for another,
found a hulking, muscled stooge.
We three went back again for more,
when they saw us coming near,
they ran fast away,
on their faces we saw fear!

But soon they found a giant,
with a desire to join them, too.
It was our turn to search one out,
we would become an ugly crew.

And so it went, until the playground
was a hulking mass of blokes.
Then my bully looked my way and said,
"Hey can't you take my jokes?"

"A joke?" I said, "What do you mean?
What do you think amusing
to push me off the swing each day.
It's me you've been abusing!"

My bully held his hand out.
We all stood there in that park.
We shook hands and made friends.
Then my bully did remark;

"Now we've enough to play a game
of ball or other teaming sports."
Then all joined in and began to play,
there were grunts and there were snorts.

And from that day on we all met,
and played together well.
A bully might become a friend,
one can never tell.

41

ANGRY SOCCER MOMS

They yell too loud from sidelines!
They seem to get real mad!
But hey, that isn't anything--
you ought to see my dad!

MY POPSICLE MELTED

Banana and root beer, icy stuff makes a summer day.
They cool you off just right, until they melt away.

DAD'S SPORTS CAR

Sitting in our garage is a very fast racecar,
I sit there in the driver's seat, pretending to go far.

One afternoon I grabbed dad's key and put it in the slot.
Pretended to start that car right up, and back it from that spot.

I revved real hard and screeched the brakes,
and drove it down the drive.
I turned about in a figure eight.
"I WILL ARRIVE ALIVE!"

I think I yelled too loudly,
got too excited to just pretend,
now my dad had heard me--
and soon my fun would end.

I'd turned the radio up real loud,
yet heard my dad's shrill shout,
"Junior, hope you're not in my car again!"
That's when I sneaked back out.

Next time I will really drive
that red sports car some more.
But now I'm too small to get out,
I can't open the door!

43

UM AND ME

Um and Me were real good friends,
they played most every day.
They were different from each other,
so diverse in every way.
Um was quiet and quite polite,
while Me was brash and loud.
They went together everywhere,
and Me would draw a crowd.

Um stayed silent, watching Me,
as Me amused young and old.
Um wondered why she was so shy,
and why Me was so bold.
Me got all the attention,
Um was overlooked, ignored.
When Um told a story
Most people acted bored.

But then one day Um spoke up--

"Me, you ought to know,
the more I hang around you,
the more I just must show.
For you are outspoken, yes, you are,
please teach me how to be."

"But Um, I like you as you are,
and the only Me is me.
We are good friends because
we are as different as can be.
If we were the same, we'd both go mad,
we'd drive each other nuts.
So let's just stay the way we are,
no ifs, no ands, no buts."

(Before you think my grammar bad, that I don't know my Me from I,
please let me explain, that Me's not me, but the name of a loud guy.
Well, you should have known that I would know, after all I know the rule,
because "Tom and I", not "Tom and me" would jump into a pool.)

TEDDY AND BLANKET

My teddy and my blanket go everywhere with me.
My little sister carts around her doll and her own blankie.
They go to all the places that we travel with our Pop.
Then one day in the grocery store, my teddy bear went PLOP!

We made it home before I knew my teddy had gone missing.
And we went back to the store, but no teddy I'd be kissing.
The store was shut tight for the night and all the lights were off.
I started crying oh so hard and then I heard a cough,
and "Ahem" and "Phew" and then a real long "Sigh."
Through the glass I saw my teddy bear, he was so close by.
He walked up to the door and opened it real wide,
teddy pushed straight through the door and hurried right outside.

And just as we were hugging, as happy as we seemed,
my Pop shook my shoulder and woke me as I dreamed.
My teddy was on my pillow just as he was each night.
"I'm so glad that you came back!" I hugged my teddy tight.

I'M AS ME AS I CAN BE

Have you ever seen a stick man?
Or one who's big and round?
Have you ever seen too-curly hair?
Or straight hair hanging to the ground?

We come in shapes and sizes
All unique as you can see.
That's why I like the way I am,
I'm as me as I can be.

AN OCEAN WAVE

While I was surfing in the ocean,
a bright fish swam by me.
He pulled me way down under,
to the bottom of the sea.

We had a great adventure,
we swam right by a shark.
I even grabbed an electric eel,
he gave me a shocking spark.

I swam back to the surface,
thought I would just hang ten.
But an ocean wave crashed into me,
and pushed me in deep again.

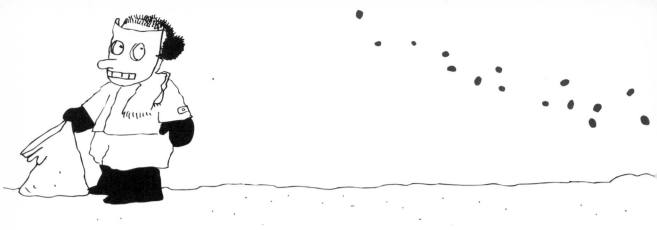

HALLOWEEN COSTUMES

I wanted to march in the parade
with a costume, oh so scary.
I worked real hard and drew a sketch
I'd have horns and be quite hairy...
My mom agreed to sew my suit,
an original for sure t'would be,
I'd win my school's costume contest,
couldn't wait for all to see.

On Halloween morn I sprang right up,
excited and all full of joy.
With my costume on I'd be so grand,
the bestest costumed boy!

But it was snowing, the wind was blowing,
so mom said, "Get your coat,
your boots, your snow pants and your gloves."
My costume dream now remote.

By the time I'd put my winter clothes on,
over my scary, hairy troll,
I looked like one big padded dork.
I'd lost my costume goal.

50

RUNAWAY SHADOW

Shadow! Shadow!
Where are you?
Without my shadow I'm so blue…
I searched down low.
Where could he be?
My shadow usually always follows me.

I searched up high, he wasn't there
I searched all over, he was nowhere.
And then down the street
I caught a sight.
My shadow was gone,
because it was night…

51

HENRY McTEVIN

There once was a boy named Henry McTevin.
He was afraid of things, mostly his brother Kevin.
He never felt brave and was never too sure.
He needed to find a total fear cure.

One day Kevin came in and said, "Henry, my brother,
if you don't climb the roof, I'm going to tell mother
about what you did to the hamster,
when you stepped and made him squeak,
and why that poor hamster never again would speak."

And though it was an accident, poor Henry felt fear,
just thinking of mom's reaction if she were to hear.
And more than his brother, Henry feared mom and dad.
He'd never do anything that they might think bad...

So he climbed and he climbed, though not supposed to,
because he'd usually do what brother said, "DO!"
And as they were climbing, Kevin slipped and fell back.
Henry caught him and held him, but alas and alack.
Kevin just slipped and then hung in the air.
Now Henry must save him, but would Henry dare?
Henry looked at a tree, then climbed out on a limb,
and pulled himself up, then he gave a large grin.
"Say, Kevin, you have had quite a scare,
so *I'm* going to save *you*, though that seems so rare."
Then Henry McTevin, leaned out and pulled hard,
helping big brother Kevin land safe back in their yard.
Since that one day, Henry McTevin's no longer afraid,
not after that heroic rescue of brother Kevin he made!

BLACK HOLE

A black hole at the end of my street
swallows bad girls and mischievous boys.

It gulps down awful dogs who bite,
bouncy balls and other toys.

I'll never, ever go near that hole
down at the end of my street...

That black hole is so hungry
I'm afraid that it's me it would eat.

CRAZY CLYDE

There once was a man
we called Crazy Clyde.

When the children came out,
old Clyde would go hide.

He'd peek from his window,
then pull down his shade.

Poor Clyde in there trembling,
kids made him afraid.

But the kids viewed it different,
they thought Clyde was weird.

They made fun of his clothes,
and his long, straggly beard.

They'd yell at him and taunt him,
poor Clyde was a mess.

When the kids would tease him,
Clyde just felt distress.

We never got to find out
if Clyde was truly weird.

Because one deep, dark night,
Clyde simply disappeared.

A GEEK, NO A FREAK

My brother calls me a geek.
My sister says, "NO, HE'S A FREAK!"

I am the youngest, I'm the runt.
No matter what I say,
both of them just grunt.

To be the smallest in the group
sometimes isn't fun at all.
I never get to be biggest,
I never am as tall.

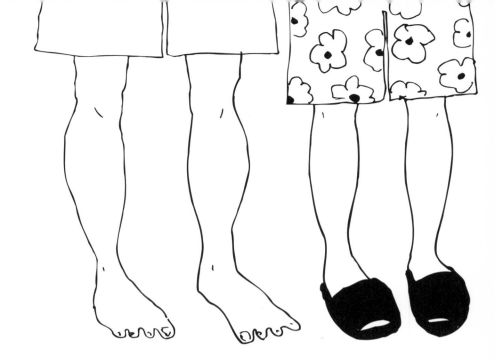

Mom says things will even out
when we all get older,
I'll have to wait 'till then, I guess,
to be bigger and bolder!

But for now I am a gopher,
I am just like their slave.
"Go get this!" my sister shrieks.
"DO THIS!" my brother'll rave.

I can't wait till we are older,
and I will be the one
who will make those two dummies
do what I want done!

MY SCHOOL LIBRARY

In our school library
are so many books for you and me.
I like to look at pictures
to see what I can see.
There are many scary stories,
adventures and romances, too.
In our school library,
there's so much for us to do.
I check out books and read some there,
I want to read them all.
I am so very happy,
there's a library down the hall...

MY GENIE

This morning as I lay in bed
something happened when I woke--
there sitting right beside me
was a genie. He then spoke;

"I can make your dreams come true,
but, you only have three wishes."
"Anything at all you've dreamed.
fly like a bird or swim like fishes?"

I thought and thought
and thought some more.
What would I really want to be?
Then I made my first wish,
to be the bestest me.

The second wish I'll keep to myself,
on the third one I'd have to wait.
For maybe someday long from now,
I'll think of something GREAT!

EXPERIENCES

I take my own experiences,
then twist them just a turn.
Then in my head a story,
will burn and burn and burn.

For instance there's Corduroy Carl,
so called for his Corduroy pants.
He once met a lovely girl
and took her to a dance.

There was holding hands and smooching,
but oh, that sounds so very gross...
let's talk about some underwear!
Yeah, that subject is real close.

You see there is no idea,
you cannot work to write.
Just keep on imagining!
You'll think of something bright.

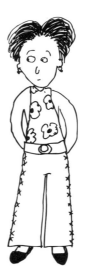

HOMEWORK

Homework, homework, it seems all I do.
Homework, homework, it makes me so blue.

I have math and reading and geography, too.
Oh homework, homework when am I through?
My teacher gives huge piles of homework to me.
I want to go play now! I want to be free!
But I have more assignments, it never seems to end.
I'm so sick of homework, but to my studies I must tend.

SPIDERS

Eight times more creepy!
Eight times as sick!
The spider spins sticky webs.
The spider crawls so quick.

But not as quickly as my skin,
which shudders at the sight
of spiders spinning down my way
when I turn off my light.

AT THE END OF THE DAY

At the end of the day, what did I do?
"Not much," I say with a yawn.
Mom asks me this question about school every day,
"Can't we just move along?
Nothing happened," I retort,
"it was just a normal day."
Dinner was almost over,
I wanted to go and play.
But momma pushed, and asked me,
to tell my normal stuff.
I thought and thought and thought
more until I'd thought enough.

And then I thought about the bus,
which carries me to school,
"Well, there was this one little thing,"
I said, "and it was kind of cool."
My dad looked up and waited for what I next would say.
"This big old dog jumped on my bus, and ran around today.
The bus driver pulled over, to try to calm him down.
Then as the bus got started he put on a big frown.
The dog jumped in the driver's seat and drove that bus away.
The bus driver had fallen out, and the dog wanted to play."

I went on and on with that tale, it grew and grew and grew.
And when I finally finished with dinner we were all through.
So now when mom asks about my day, I add some details, too.
To make it much more interesting about things that I go do.

CRISS CROSS, APPLESAUCE

My teacher said, "You must sit still and listen very well."

"Criss your arms and cross your legs!"

"But my feet, they really smell!"

"Now don't be silly!" teacher said.
"Criss and cross your legs to stay."

Then put her finger to her lips.
That's all I learned today.

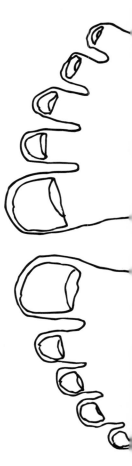

TURTLENECK

M
o
m
makes
me wear
this sweater.
It's too narrow
at the top. I pull it
on my body, then off
my neck it pops. It is so
tight up by my neck, oh, what a
face I make. A turtle never strangles.
Should've called this shirt a snake!

CHOCOLATE COVERED FROG LEGS

Chocolate covered frog legs
go hopping off my plate.

I better run and catch them,
or my breakfast will be late.

Just when I thought I had them,
they sprung and sproing and sprang.

I better catch those frog legs
to feed my breakfast gang.

I sneaked beneath the table.
I crept across the floor.

I watched those frog legs jump around,
then hop right out the door.

So, I guess I'll have some waffles,
or other breakfast eats.

But chocolate covered frog legs
are my favorite breakfast treats!

WEIRD NEIGHBORS

I have so many neighbors,
with a new one on the way.
The lady just next door to us
has another due today.

She has eighteen kids already,
they make up half our block!
It gets really loud over there
when they all start to talk.

The guy who lives across the street
mows the lawn in a long dress.
Why he does that I don't know,
it's anybody's guess.

Oh, I could go on for quite awhile
about my neighbors, oh so weird.
Perhaps later I will tell you,
about the lady with a beard!

Oh, neighbors are quite funny.
Some repel and some delight!
But I won't mention the scary man,
who comes out in the night...

TREES

My backyard is so full of trees
in springtime they all make me sneeze.
      Some are short and some are tall,
      some turn colors in the fall.
            I like to hang from all those trees,
            though they sometimes skin my knees.
                  A tree is great for shade and climbs,
                  and trees are great to use in rhymes.
                        So find a tree and climb up high.
                        So high you'll be up in the sky.
                              If you don't have a backyard tree,
                              go to the park and you will see.

72

A BAD TREE POEM PUN

Branch out now, don't leaf me out.
When your dog barks, a bud might sprout.

    Now we're getting to the root of it.
    Under a tree, I love to sit.

        But this makes no earthly sense.
        So this poem is now past tense.

DINKY SPOON

Most kids have something special,
a teddy, pillow or a blankie.
I too have something
without which I become quite cranky.
Seems now I have lost it,
I'm feeling so sad.
Everyone's looking for him,
both my mom and my dad.
Dinky spoon, dinky spoon,
where have you been?
When I find you, I will begin to grin.
I'll hold you close, right near my heart.
And from you never more will I part.
My dinky spoon's perfect for eating ice cream,
and it helps me with cereal just like a dream.
On the handle is my dinky spoon friend,
a tiny dinosaur right there on the end.
His name is dinky,
he lives on a spoon.
And now I've misplaced him,
I better find him real soon.
Because lunch is a'coming,
and I need him to eat.
Dinky Spoon where are you?
Come, let's go find a treat!

CHEESY

The word describes the way I feel
about someone who's absurd.
Another way to say it is,
he's a goof or he's a nerd.

A cheesy person is the worst
kind of silly sort.
A cheesy person always laughs
and lets out a big snort.

I never want to be cheesy
because it isn't good.
I never want to be cheesy,
and I doubt you ever would.

Burgers should be cheesy,
but people should not be.
The biggest kind of geek
is one who is cheesy!

CAR ALARMS

When we are at the airport
or in a mall's parking lot
we lose our own car.
Now which lane? Seems we just forgot.

Then mom presses on her car key,
and our car beeps and blinks.
We find our car out there then.
Now that is smart of mom methinks.

A SONG

A song can make you happy.
A song can make you sad.

A special song can make you sing
to your mom or dad.

The song I like goes:
BOOM, BOOM, BOOM,

AYEEEE! and then a CHEER.
Mom and dad don't like that one--

"TURN IT DOWN, THAT HURTS MY EAR!"

A ROOF OVER YOUR HEAD

"It's cold and now it's blowing,"
my father always would say.
My mom played along with him,
"And how much snow today?".

She'd heard it all before.
His weather lecture du jour.
But one more time
she'd hear it.
Another snow she would endure.

"'Tis a good night for a roof
over one's own head.
When it's cold and snowy
you have a warm bed."

My dad always says that
when the weather turns cold.
"It's a good night to have a roof over your head!"
And now you've all been told.

LIGHTNING AND THUNDER

Under my bed
is where you will find me
when it rains and it rumbles.
No lightning will I see.

My doggie too is scared,
so I must protect her.
We hide under the bed,
and I stroke her soft fur.

The lightning and the thunder
make me wonder why and where.
Is it bowling or is it golf
the angels play up there?

ANOTHER BOOGIE MAN

In my hall closet
and under my bed
is the boogie man guy--
but he's all in my head.

See, he doesn't exist.
If he did we'd be friends.
Some think he'd be scary,
I say it depends.

He might be the frightened one
with no one to talk to and share.
Maybe if someone just met him,
they would both start to care.

But for now I'll just keep him
in my imagination and my head,
I won't try to meet or greet him,
as he sleeps under my bed.

MY SHORTS ARE LOOSE

My brother took my underwear
by accident I guess.
I am much smaller than he
with a bad wedgie he is dressed.
But, laundry day's tomorrow,
and was down to my last pair.
How am I supposed to wear these things?
How can I wear his underwear?
They fit me like a hammock,
I could swing in them you see.
That gives me a great idea--
I'll just hang them in our tree.

84

ROCK CANDY

My sister had a box of rocks,
she said they tasted swell.
I watched her crunch and chew one,
and thought our mom I'd tell.
Your teeth are hard and chew well.
But, candy made of rocks?
You might as well eat motor parts,
and parts of grandpa's clocks.
Why would they make this candy,
from rocks and hard, hard stuff?
I would think you'd break your teeth,
and that would be real tough.

WHAT'S ON TV?

What's on TV?
I'm so bored!
Looks like my team
might just have scored.
Turn the channel.
Hear a tune.
And find out what
to plant in June.
Then on to animals
in the deepest jungle.
Without the television,
I'd sit and mumble.

PUBERTY BUMMERS

Oh no, that's a zit!
The same with that one there!
Why is it my face breaks out now
where once it didn't dare?
And now my voice is changing too,
it modulates and slips.
This puberty's a bummer,
I've got to get a grip!

MY BLANKIE

It's tattered and it's old,
it's seen a better day.
My blankie is my favorite thing,
it's still better than okay!
I keep what's left in my pocket,
though it used to be quite nice.
I've loved my favorite blankie so!
So now I'll squeeze it twice.

CAR AIR FRESHENERS

On the mirror is a pine tree
that swings and smells so good.
It keeps the car from stinking.
It's like we're in the woods.

CHEESEBURGERS REVISITED

Mustard and ketchup,
mayo and a pickle and barbecue sauce -
Oh my fancy they tickle. And thick buns with seeds,
the sesame kind, and burgers so juicy, the thickest ones you can find.
A cheeseburger surprise, oh, a double is great!
Can't stop thinking about cheeseburgers! They are really first rate!
So meet me for lunch, or for breakfast or dinner.
If they have cheeseburgers,
that will be a WINNER!

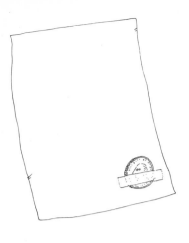

I FOUND A QUARTER

I found a quarter, picked it up,
attached was a small letter.
"If you should find my quarter,
I hope you use it better.
I knew that I would lose it,
that's why I wrote this note.
I tied it to a nice long string,
which hung around my throat.
My quarter sure was special.
It is one alike no other.
This quarter wasn't really mine.
I took it from my brother."

JAMIE JAMMY

Jamie Jammy likes his jelly.
Says with bread it fills his belly.
He slathers it on so very thick.
Eats it down, so very quick.

IF I HAD A MILLION DOLLARS

If I had a million dollars,
my life would change, oh yes.
I'd find so many ways to spend
I'd clean up a big mess.
I'd try to solve world hunger,
I'd find a cure for stuff,
within an hour it'd be gone,
and that would be so rough.
A million won't go very far,
with goals as big as mine.
That's why a kid my age,
gets an allowance -- and that's fine!

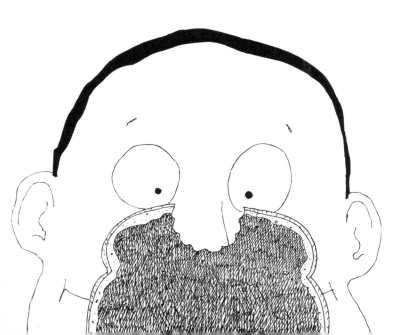

FIZZY POP AND SUGAR CANDY

Snacks of sugar taste so good!
I could eat them all the day!
They don't do much for my body.
But sometimes that's okay.

OLD HALLOWEEN CANDY

I hid my Halloween candy,
so well that it is lost.
Have you seen my pillowcase full of loot?
Can you guess what it would cost?
What happened, I can't imagine,
it used to be right here.
I hid my Halloween candy,
I'll never find it now I fear.
I think my dog must have eaten it,
or I hid it really well.
I miss my bag of candy.
If you knew where, would you tell?

SPORTSHEAD

A football, a puck,
a ball and a bat!
A cheering crowd,
now, that's where it's at!
    When I'm at the ballpark
    and crisp is in the air
    I'm lost in my sports,
    I don't have a care.
        The fans all go nuts,
        the stands just explode.
        It is so much fun
        to be in a sports mode.
            I'm having such fun,
            it's where I want to be!
            And not too long from now,
            you'll all cheer for ME!

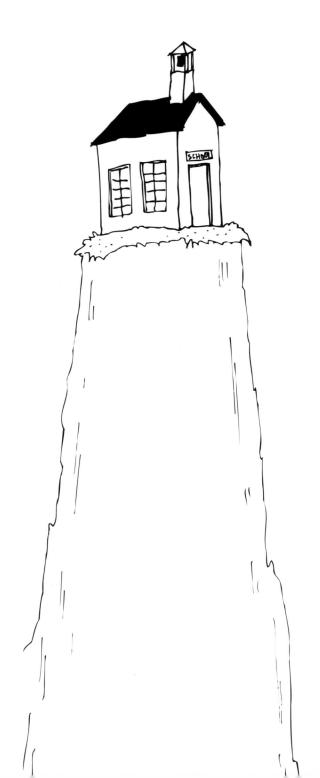

THE OLDEN DAYS

My aunt was talking about back when she walked to school.
She made it sound uphill both ways, but I am not a fool.

I know she had a school bus then, just like my daddy did.
Because he was her brother, when they were both a kid.

She told me how so very hard it was with no television shows.
But dad has told me stories, and this is how it goes:

"When I was your age it was hard. We didn't have so much.
We didn't have a telephone. We wrote to keep in touch.

We didn't have an automobile to drive us all 'bout town.
We didn't have much food to eat, which made poor grandpa frown.

Oh times were hard in the olden days. The world was black and white.
I guess you've heard of all the wars. Just why do people fight?"

Well mom walked in and shook her head, and told him not to fib.
They aren't that old to remember this, their stories are ad lib.

They actually grew up in a house, with modern stuff back then.
They always story-tell so much, of what they call "back when".

But grandpa, that's another story. Now, he has some things to say.
But his stories all go on and on. We'll save them for another day.

FOUR EYES

When I was only in fourth grade
(now that seems so long ago),
I had to get some glasses,
though I said a loud "NO!"
I wore what looked like goggles,
thick frames wrapped all in black.
I didn't like the way I looked
I wanted a head sack.
But when I looked at my first tree
with clearer vision true,
I saw the leaves were separate
and the sky was dark and blue.
So even though I looked real dumb
in my glasses what a goof--
I saw things with those glasses
of which before I had no proof.

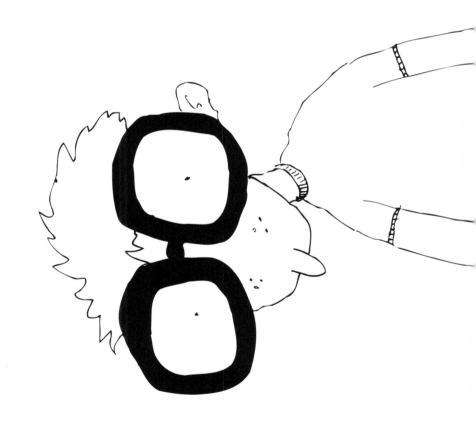

FOOTBALL SEASON

I like to watch a football game,
sitting in dad's chair, surely.
We shout and yell at the screen
when our team does poorly.

The game goes back and forth sometimes,
but we root together all the way!
We watch our favorite football team
and wish they played each day.

With some popcorn and some peanuts
and snacks which taste so fine,
the day spent watching football
with my dad is just divine!

WHAT'S DOWN THERE?

I dug a hole to China.
You should see what all I've seen.
There are many, many people
and their trees are the same green.

People looked at me down there
as I climbed out of my hole.
I dug a hole to China,
and slid down a long pole.

I had to climb back out of there,
it took one hundred years!
I guess I've pushed my tale too far.
Don't believe all that you hear.

103

POLKA-DOT SOAP

My polka-dot soap hangs on a rope
it has vibrant great colors galore!
I use it each day, and it smells really okay
but there's always less, never more.

It melts when I use it.
I hate to abuse it.
It's pretty and clean in my bath.
It puts dots on my skin.
The boys at school will all grin.
"SHE HAS POLKA DOT MEASLES!
CLEAR A PATH!"

THE IMAGINATOR

There once was a writer
who lived down in a cave.

He was the Imaginator,
but his friends just called him Dave.

"An Imaginator imagines
all sorts of fun things--
aliens and princes,
cowboys and kings!"

An Imaginator magically
turns thoughts into truth.
Come to his cave with me today
and you'll see the proof.

A REAL FISHY STORY

One fish,
two fish,
fish guts,
phew fish!

I'm not going to eat it!
That would be too smelly.
It would make me feel so bad,
sitting in my belly.

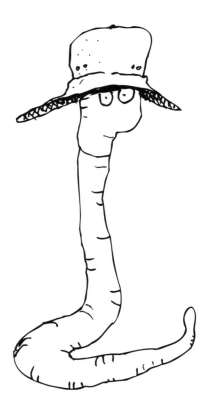

As I threw that fish back,
I heard him yell out,
"That smell you are smelling
is not from this trout!
That smell you are smelling
comes from your own hat,
The worm you just hooked
is named Little Pat.
He got stuck on your hat hooks,
and he is a stinky sort.
I would not suggest,
you leave Pat there!"
he said with a fish snort.

Well, this is a fish story,
and they're usually all just fiction
I mean, do you think a fish
uses words or any diction?

GIRAFFES

A giraffe has spots and a very long neck.
He eats the leaves where birds can peck.
He chews real loud and stoops way down.
He's the tallest animal in my town.

I have a giraffe living in my yard,
he plays with me, he's quite a card.
He has to bend down when I deal,
and when he wins he gives a squeal.
A squeal so loud it hurts my ears.
And wait until you hear his cheers.
He's tall and loud and smells at times,
but he is fun when we go on climbs.
He lifts me into the tallest tree,
my giraffe is a very good friend to me.

JACK AND JILL?

It was actually Jack Horner who lived on that hill.
He lived up there with his sister Jill.
They had a job, to fill a pail.
They knew they could, they'd never fail.

So they set their course, up the hill they both went,
they tumbled to the bottom, but to no real lament.
They dusted themselves off and headed back up,
and that part of the story I have just made up.

A BOOK

Sometimes I read a story, and imagine I am there.
I tune out all the other things. I just don't have a care.
I curl up near my pillow, with my special nighttime light.
Some nights I read a funny one. Some nights I read a fright!
A book is a companion to take you far away.
You can read about adventures, in the night or in the day.

MR. GREEN'S HOUSE

For years I have heard
about Mr. Green's house,
that it might be haunted,
by his long-lost spouse.
We ride bikes by slowly,
as the sun's getting low.
Mr. Green's garage
has a spooky glow.
Some of the older kids
claim they heard a lady growl
as they ran up Mr. Green's drive,
when they were on a prowl.
They all said they saw her
hiding in Mr. Green's dark place.
I wouldn't be surprised at all,
to see a creepy face.
I'm not sure I believe it's true,
or that it could even be.
But I keep my mind open
to things I cannot see.
Mr. Green seems very sad,
like he'd like to have a guest.
I think I'll go up and see him.
Perhaps tomorrow would be best?

SCUBA DUDE

With flippers on my feet
and an air tank on my back,
I dove into the water,
deep down where blue's blue-black.

Down there I saw fish and things
with teeth as long as me,
and sharper than a needle,
just as scary as can be.

I found a ship that had gone down
while full of gold and stuff.
I tried to lug it to the top,
but tugging it was tough!

I motioned to my buddy,
and bubbled, "Hlbbb mee ouuut!"
He pointed to his air tank,
and gave a bubble-shout,

"Wee needdd to get uppp toooo the topppp!
Wee cannot bbbbreath dddown herrrre."
We swam above the wreck and many fish,
black to blue and then to clear.

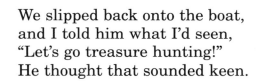

We slipped back onto the boat,
and I told him what I'd seen,
"Let's go treasure hunting!"
He thought that sounded keen.

Back down below we both went,
this time there was a treasure guard.
A shark seemed to like that loot too
down in that deep boat yard.

So we left it all alone
and found a safer place.
I like to scuba with a friend
with a mask upon my face!

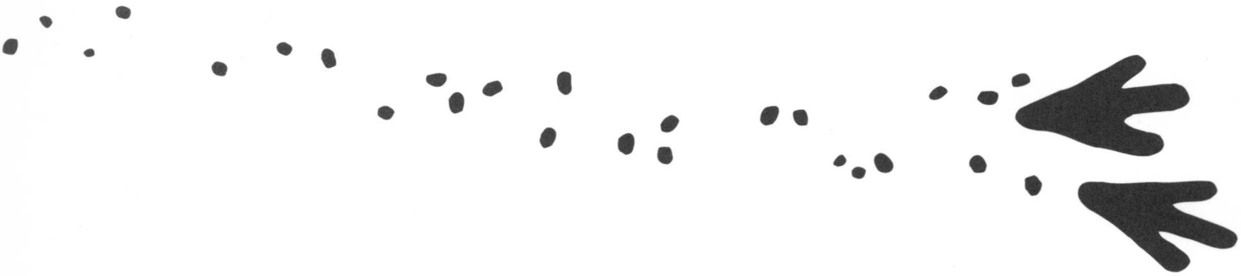

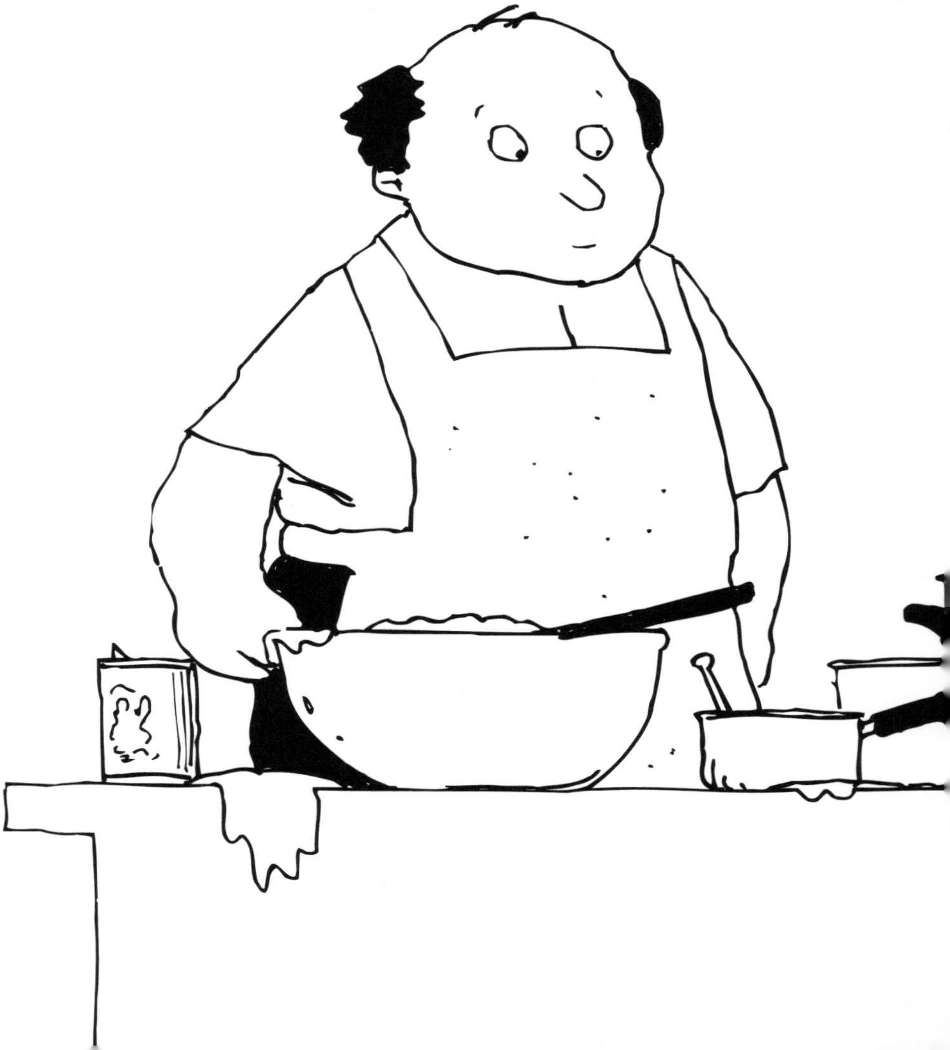

MY COOKBOOK

My kitchen cookbook sits on a high nook, just waiting for me to come in.
I look to my ma, then to my pa. "May I cook?" They both grin.
We get down the book, each starts to fix a favorite thing.
As we are cooking and preparing a meal, the phone starts to ring.
"It's grandma and it's grandpa, we're coming there for dinner!"
"That's great!" I say, "and tonight we've cooked a winner!"
When they come, we have such fun, and everything is tasty.
Cooking with your family's fun, but please don't try be too hasty.

UNDERPANTS DANCE

When underpants dance
you better jump out of your pants
cuz they wiggle and waggle each way
they'll catch you and jump
right off of your rump
and chase you all night and all day

when they hop and they creep
you might just be asleep
while they secretly prance
they move fast in the dark
they can run through a park
in their odd underpants dance

underpants all have a mind of their own
hold on to them tight or they will go roam…

*(An odd poem suggested to Matott by first graders
while at lunch one day. That explains it, huh?)*

THE MYSTERIOUS PAIR

Once there was a tighty-white
who came out only at night,
jumped right out of my dresser drawer.
It danced around quick,
oh, what a great pair to pick,
and now you'll want to hear more.

A WEDGIE

I grabbed hard and pulled
I ripped his underwear
I ran away really fast,
in my hand I had the pair.
My big, ugly brother,
screamed 'cuz he was mad,
"You got the wrong pair you dork!
You pulled them off poor dad!"

BABY T-REX

I'm a little T-Rex,
short and stout.
Here are my teeth,
and here is my snout.
When I get real hungry,
you can hear me shout,
"I'll eat you up
and poop you out."

BOOGER MINER

While sitting in my car one day at a stoplight I got ill
from what I watched there next to me while our cars were very still.
I was staring at this young guy who was mining in his nose.
Way up to his second knuckle! Wondered just how far he goes.
I tried to look away, but was captivated well.
How could this guy sit there and pick? On this subject I must dwell.

Did he not see me watching while he sat there in his car?
He pushed in even deeper, now he had gone too far!
His hand was disappearing, how does he fit it in?
He was glancing right my way, I thought I saw him grin.
On my face there was a grimace, I thought I might be sick.
You'd think when he knew I watched, he'd pull his hand out quick.
But his face then held a grimace, the same as mine I guess.
Watching him picking his nose could make me faint I must confess.
But he seemed more determined. Something up there must come out!
He tugged and pulled and picked so hard, I'd wave my hand, and shout,

120

"HEY, YOU ARE DISGUSTING!
YOUR WINDOW'S MADE OF GLASS!
CAN'T YOU SEE ME WATCHING?"
HE WAVED HIS HAND TO PASS.

The stoplight had turned to green, he drove with just one fist.
The other hand still up his nose-- must have been one there he missed.
We pulled up to the next stoplight, him still mining in his schnoz.
No one should do that in public. Yes, we ought to pass some laws.

A lady pulled up next to me, her face crinkled in disgust.
She thought it was revolting too. He should stop now, he just must.
But, now his wrist was up his nose, a disgusting thing to see.
Then I was shocked by my reflection. That miner guy was me!

INDEX, 122

WELL, THAT'S IT

What a waste of paper, some of you might have thunk.
Why did he write down all that stuff? That last one really stunk!
I could do better than that! *I* could write a better poem!
And so we invite just that. Please, let your mind now roam.
Included after this bad poem, is blank paper just for you--
I have a plan, a great idea. So here is what you do:
Write out your poem and draw a sketch, copy it real nice.
Then send it to the address here, please lick the envelope twice.
And put a stamp and address on the front before you mail.
And we will read it with the rest, and you might just prevail.
Oh, and don't forget the disclaimer with the poem and sketch you send,
we need to know your parents know, their approval they must lend.
Underwear is THE thing, a favorite idea for Matott!
He wants to do an undie book, in case you just forgot...
Your name will go next to your poem, published with Matott and Woods.
We hope you like the idea. We hope you have the goods.
We might just edit them a bit, Matott might add a line,
to make the poems and drawings GREAT! We all must revise and refine.

Do you have a poem and/or a drawing for Mr. Matott and Mr. Woods's next anthology
of poems, or a really great name for the book (After *There's A Fly On My Toast!*
and *Chocolate Covered Frog Legs* we need a good one)? We are thinking of
DRAIN BAMAGE, what do you think of that? Please send your ideas to:

SKOOB BOOKS
C/O MATOTT/WOODS
PO Box 261183
Littleton, CO 80163

RIBBET! RIBBET!
What Up, Frog?